W9-ASN-297

Mary Had a Dinosaur

Published in 2009 by Windmill Books, LLC
303 Park Avenue South, Suite # 1280, New York, NY 10010-3657

Series Editor: Nick Turpin
Design: Robert Walster
Production: Jenny Mulvanny

Publisher Cataloging Data

Browne, Eileen
        Mary had a dinosaur / Eileen Browne and Ruth Rivers.
                p. cm. – (Get ready)
        Summary: Simple rhyming text and colorful illustrations tell about the day
Mary's dinosaur goes to school.
        ISBN 978-1-60754-262-9
        1. Dinosaurs—Juvenile fiction   2. Schools—Juvenile fiction   [1. Dinosaurs—Fiction
2. Schools—Fiction   3. Stories in rhyme]   I. Rivers, Ruth   II. Title   III. Series
        [E]—dc22

Manufactured in the United States of America

Mary Had a Dinosaur

Eileen Browne
and Ruth Rivers

alphabet
soup

an imprint of

WINDMILL
BOOKS
New York

Mary had a…

...dinosaur,

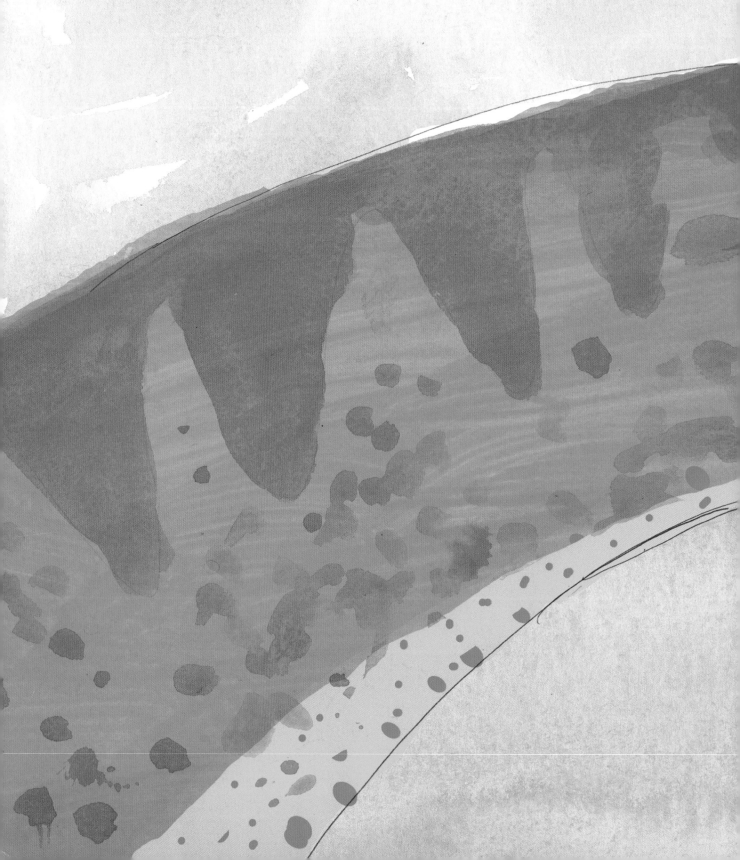

with horns…

...and spotty knees.

It shared her lunch,

it pushed her swing...

...it helped her
climb some
trees.

16

It followed her…

...to school one day.

The children said,

22

23

25

It made the children laugh...

...to see a dinosaur...

...in school!

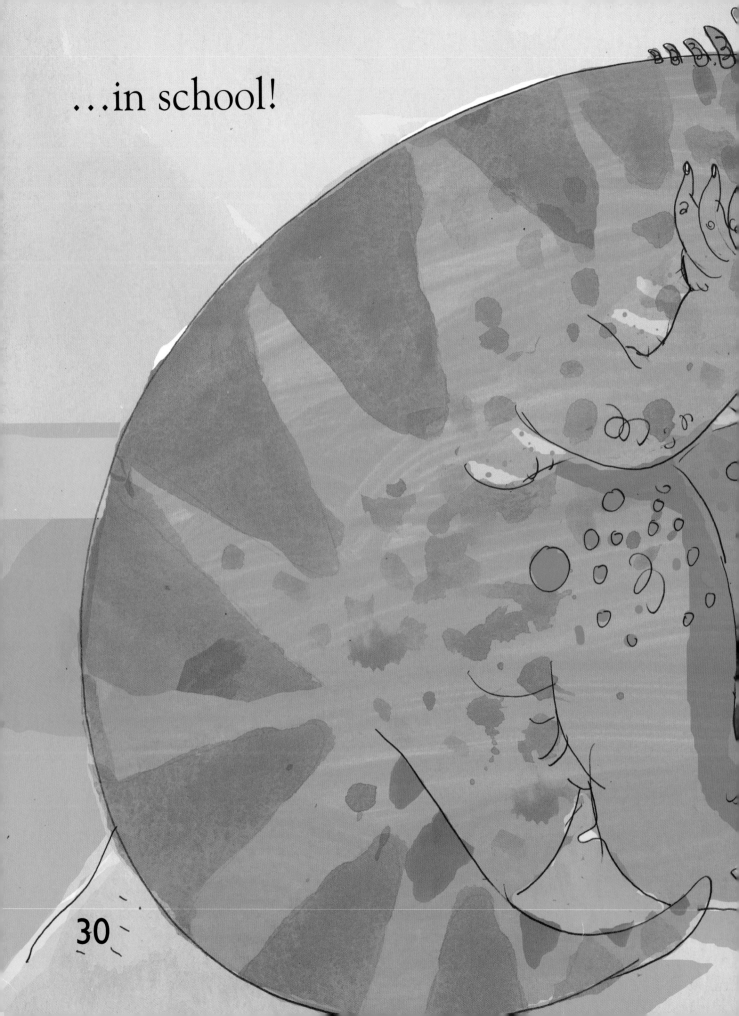